My Soviet Union

My Soviet Union

Michael Dumanis

University of Massachusetts Press *Amherst*

LC 2007003920
ISBN 978-1-55849-585-2

Designed by Sally Nichols
Set in Granjon
Printed and bound by Sheridan Books, Inc.

Library of Congress Cataloging-in-Publication Data

Dumanis, Michael, 1976–
  My Soviet Union / Michael Dumanis.
      p. cm.
  "Winner of the 2006 Juniper Prize for Poetry"—
  ISBN 978-1-55849-585-2 (pbk. : alk. paper)
  1. Soviet Union—Poetry. I. Title.
  PS3604.U46M9 2007
  811'.6—dc22

                        2007003920

British Library Cataloguing in Publication data are available.

for my sisters, Maria and Sonya

Hey!
Ladies and gentlemen!
Lovers
of sacrilege,
crimes,
carnage—
have you seen
the worst horror of all—
my face,
when
I
am utterly calm?

—Vladimir Mayakovsky, 1893–1930

ACKNOWLEDGMENTS

Many thanks to the editors of journals where the following poems have previously appeared, occasionally as reprints or in slightly altered form:

Alaska Quarterly Review	"Professional Extra"
American Letters & Commentary	"Directions to the Brothel"; "Kwashiorkor"
Black Warrior Review	"Quarantine"; "Side Effect in B-minor"
Born Magazine	"Directions to the Brothel"
The Canary	"Baku, 1980"; "West Des Moines"
Chelsea	"Travel Advisory"
Columbia Poetry Review	"Tourist"; "When I Was Pol Pot"
Conduit	"Revisionist History"
Crazyhorse	"Today, on the Obituary Channel"
CutBank	"Restraint"
Denver Quarterly	"Joseph Cornell, with Box"; "Veteran"
Epoch	"The Death of Elegy"; "Gold Rush"; "Pompeii"
Hayden's Ferry Review	"The Refraction"
Indiana Review	"Memoir"; "The Rainy Season"; "We Require an Assertion of Value, We Are Frightened"
Jacket	"All the Greatest Stories Ever Told"; "Rookie"
LIT	"Life with Garcia Marquez on Long Island"
Mudfish	"Infirmary"
New England Review	"Ode"
New Orleans Review	"The Frustrated Vaudevillian"
Phoebe	"The Ordered Mind in the Disordered House"
Pleiades	"The Woods Are Burning"
Post Road	"Crime Spree"; "My Mayakovsky"
Prairie Schooner	"Banishment"; "Cancer Is a Disease of Animals"
Salt Hill	"Psalm"
Seneca Review	"Buffalo Elegies, 1982–1991"; "Certain Things"

The Texas Review	"Joseph Cornell, with Box"
Verse	"All the Greatest Stories Ever Told"; "Rookie"
Washington Square	"The Age of Reason"; "The Bouvet Øya Lighthouse Keeper Speaks After Protracted Silence"

Special thanks to Rick Barot, Erica Bernheim, Jericho Brown, Oni Buchanan, Josh Edwards, James Allen Hall, Ilya Kaminsky, Sabrina Orah Mark, Cate Marvin, ZZ Packer, Robyn Schiff, Salvatore Scibona, Nick Twemlow, and G. C. Waldrep for their encouragement, advice, and steadfast friendship.

Also grateful to Olena Kalytiak Davis, Mark Doty, Edward and Nadya Dumanis, Jorie Graham, Ed Hirsch, Rodney Jones, Mark Levine, Cynthia Macdonald, Steve Orlen, Claudia Rankine, Mark Strand, Susan Wood, and Dean Young for the meaningful conversations they had with me about poetry.

The writing of this book was made possible in part through the generous support of the University of Iowa Writers' Workshop, the University of Houston, Nebraska Wesleyan University, The Bread Loaf Writers' Conference, a Fulbright Fellowship, a Writers' Residency at The Corporation of Yaddo, a James Michener Fellowship, and C. Glenn Cambor and Progression Fellowships from Inprint, Inc.

And I am indebted to Amber Dermont, for everything she's read and said, her faith and patience.

CONTENTS

My Soviet Union

A Children's Song Adapted from the Russian

There was a landowner
who had a dog and he loved her:
she once ate a piece of meat
and he killed her.

He killed her and he buried her,
and on the headstone, wrote,
There was a landowner
who had a dog and he loved her.

ONE

The Woods Are Burning

I thought there was a war on. I was wrong. To think the war
was over me! The war was over. No: the war was over
there, the other side of the barbed wire enclosure
from our side, warless, where we fidgeted and held
each other's hands as though they were the last
we'd ever think to hold, all the while keeping
strict tabs on the body count covering the soft
field of lamb's ear, beside the nasturtiums,
it's just a field, merely an empty space
between the hydrangea bushes. The war was not over
the bushes, who, like the lamb's ear, the boy-gardener,
and the flowers, became the war's first casualties.
Because there was no cause for war and none of us
were sure there was a war for us to win, the newspapers
named it The Casual War, The War That's Not Really
a War, The Don't Mention It War, The What War,
The There Isn't a War War, The War Over Nothing,
and (on the day the papers were shut down) The War
The Authorities Ban Us From Covering. I,
as I have told the Truth Commission, didn't think
there was a war, nor spread the vicious rumor,
until the ground shook and I saw you fall, until I took
the survivor's cracked mouth into my open mouth,
tried giving the survivor my last breath, and in the smoke
and cannonfire confusion of the war, mistook
his breath for mine, and pulled (I didn't mean to) his
last breath into my healthy mouth and watched him not
survive—
                    but this is not about me. I have testified.
Lay prostrate on the courtroom floor. Went down
before the Justice of the Peace on my trick knee.
Reached for the lavender-scented sleeve of her black robe
in her secluded chamber. Swore I knew nothing of
the Schlieffen Plan, the Bay of Pigs, the secret pact

we struck to fan the cease-fire's flames until it burned
itself out of existence, as she turned to me and ran
her satin hands over my eyelids, toward my lips.
Knowing the war would never end, we kissed.

Am I the one who suffered? Was I there?

This is not about me, Trojan Horse.

2. The Insurrection

My students are angry. Biting their lips at me, brushing stray eyelashes
off with one hand's middle finger. I made them read the entirety of
Death of a Salesman out loud while I watched them. Each time the
student playing Willy Loman would say, "The woods are burning,"
I would stop her, and ask, "What woods? Why burning?" She said
Willy was one crazy son-of-a-bitch spouting gibberish mixed with
self-pity. Said his family should be relieved and grateful that he killed
himself, spared them additional anguish, more maudlin burning
forests of self-pity. I asked my students what it means for somebody
to say the woods are burning. The consensus was maybe it doesn't
mean anything. Until another student, the one playing Happy, said
he was in a forest fire once, on the periphery. "It's hard to get out of
the woods when they burn," Happy told me. "It's not like a house
fire, where you have sprinklers and smoke detectors, windows and
ladders. You can't contain it. Winds decide its course. Once it starts,
there's no stopping it. Often you don't find what started it. And when
you do, it's something insignificant, a cigarette thrown down at the
wrong angle, a heap of twigs during a dry hot season." "This play is
horrible," said Willy Loman. "Maybe in the old days, people could
relate to it. But nowadays how could you feel sorry? I had several
options: I chose not to take them. I cheated on my wife. I lived a
lie. I'm just a loser: I deserved to die." She is a beautiful woman
with bangs wearing a baby blue baby-T. She works the night shift at
the Emergency Ward, has to leave every class period a few minutes
early so she can check the wounded in on time, call the appropriate
insurance companies.

The wounded come on time to be checked in.

The wound in opposition
                    to the idea of the wound—

The woods are burning.

3. The Cinema

I had two options at the movie theater:

    1)   Footage of people being blown to pieces
    2)   Footage of people being blown

4. The Woods

    either:

It's Pilsner Time at the Palace of Tines
in Palestine, along the Seine,
where Paul Celan, that Philistine,
where Paul Celan, in pale soutane,
or someone else I once saw drown
(it was this summer, in the Seine)
is passing time. Or pausing time.

      or:

don't know
downtown
don't now
tone down

gauze gaze Gaza ghazal gazelle Giselle guise guess gasp grasp graze grace
glossary glacier glazier glass lipgloss galoshes goulashes gouaches Gauloises
valse triste the valises of Lillian Gish

gaze, gaze, Gazelle
at Giselle's disguise

a striking resemblance to
Lillian Gish

she is in Gaza now
gasping through gauze

go, go, Giselle
through Gaza's gossamer

applying your lipgloss
and grasping at air

dance, veiled Giselle,
dance the valse triste in Gaza

while the gazelles, they graze:

something like grace
that one would not call grace

your gaze assuages
I am not a carpenter

no one in my family or yours
has ever been a carpenter

Giselle, disguised,
find something in your glossary

of gazes to assuage
each gasp in Gaza

each gasp is a palette of grays

4½. The Insurrection, Continued

I don't remember things the way I used to.

Words disappear: I asked my students what apartheid was.

All of them knew,
except the ones who were black.

None of my students were black.

I asked my students what Jim Crow was.

None of them knew, except the students
who were black.

I tried comparing Jim Crow to apartheid,
but that's like saying that the circumstances of my sister's murder
were like the circumstances of your sister's murder.

I have no sisters.

True or False? Lillian Gish

True or False? Paul Celan

Fatty Arbuckle? I ask my students.

They don't know.

They, who know everything.

Are the woods burning?

What time is it anyway?

No, I have hundreds of sisters.
Most of them died in the war.

5. The Eulogy

these are the only
remains of your circus

fat dwarves emerging
from the thin hour

this dancing camel and his
indiscernible strings

this photogravure
of the wild man of borneo

this is your borneo
this backwoods laughter

you've bent over backwards
you're stilted on stilts

you're highly unlikely
inside this enclosure

this ring is the zero
sum game of your passion

this maudlin this dusk
this unpurchased concession

this leotard's seam tear
this falling of limbs

this cobweb the only
thing veiling your laughter

this would-be obscured
trap of doorway and these

various passions of clowns
along with them the memory

of riding a train
through a forest on fire

then passing the fire
and seeing the platform

and leaving the train

One

I am in love with Johnny, because he *does* love me,
and I am in love with Stanley, because he will *never* love me,
and Thorvald, whose uncle carved icebergs off Norway,
were I to fall for Salvo, we'd move to Italy,
and with my locksmith, she is rough, she's short on money,
am I in love with Kattrin, who has made herself mute,
Dolores, I love you, the pain in your name,
dear Mindy, because you seem pie-faced and sweet, make me tea,
let me molest the rose mole in the cleft of your chin,
and let me molest, on your back, every sinkhole, each nodule,
I'll reconceive all these as what, reaffirmations,
and I am in love yes I am with my childhood's squat flat,
and with the *Rubaiyat of Omar Khayyam*, which I chose not to read,
but could not put down on account of its red leather binding.

Two

This country is so thin and worn that we
can see each other through it, and I love
how you are thus aware that I, however threadbare
I might have become, am still here,
and I am in love with myself, for how can
I not be and still be, and I love the loud rain,
it means water, and also the cross in the churchyard,
it signifies what, history, and how I miss every movie
I've seen, even *Delousing Alfred*, even, I trust, *Ramming Paige*,
they comprise my itinerary, and I am in love with the cranes,
metal and tall on Sicilian hills, which both Salvo and I one still dawn
from one aperture in a small inn, thought were crosses,
O Fantasies, O Signs of Always Progress.
Later, I spent too much time in a city,

Three

I really enjoyed it, I felt almost holy inside it,
there were some orchids I contrived to be.

You have sex then you are sweaty
You have grief you use it wisely
You have eyes each eye has cruelties
Guinea pigs they up and leave you
CAT scans cats which phone is ringing
You have stuff it gives you duties

(You have many duties some may involve torture or parties)

You have words then also lonely
You have dark you have always
You have death so they tell you
You have breath and the faces of babies
You were once inside you along with whatever
The names are of cavities organs

(You have tacks and staples you have dreams about them)

You have many digits you spend hours counting
You have two arms they are the last longings
You have words some are in Sanskrit
You have words what are their colors
You have words how are they meaning
You have world you have lovely

(You have many quarrels with nudes world and lovely)

You have nudes have you unholy
You have a nude whose body has you
You have what a body how you try to hide in it
You have obscene you have your parents
Your parents have nothing your parents who had you
Except for the day you were born on the day

(You have not and for which you refuse to forgive them)

You have horns you have a word-hole
You have a mouthwash you never use it
You have leprosy have lockjaw

Have black lung disease or will soon
You have mining but no pickaxe
But no deposits no lantern

(Although you have many coupons including a heap of expired ones)

Have location is this Pitt Street
You have east of Westside Highway
Have a surface surface has you
Have a compass does it function
Have a sphere and on occasion hiccups
You have water and it sometimes masks them

(Although a prayer lumps of bread and a yawn have once or twice
    proven useful)

Have reconcile have God Almighty
Have enough it will not please you
You have nothing others wish for
You have wishing for what have they
You have writhing have also misleading directions
To the brothel where you have decided

There might be bounty, further possessions

Sadly, I came upon
more than one Greene Street.

Sadly, I tailed
the all-wrong Mr. S.

I would have done.
I plotted to have done.

Forgot that order mattered.
Mixed up days.

I swear I did not mean
the knife to slip,

the slip to give,
each fruitcart to turn over.

Did not intend
the epileptic fit

in the hushed theater.
Am so sorry for.

And swear to God.
And was so whisper-close.

And then I wasn't.
Crouching in the Den

of Mirrored Surfaces,
beside myself,

I found myself
unable to discern.

Mistakes were made
with pupils, fingertips.

A half-assed grope.
A fondle. I grew fond,

I came to fall for you,
must go now. Bearing,

like an old steamer trunk,
these bouts of breathing,

I am in no position
to stay put,

even in wartorn Milwaukee.
In cotton candy Beirut.

Even in Krakow,
an affectless climate,

the jukebox won't cease
playing polkas.

The final Yum Yum Shoppe has closed its doors:
pray tell, where can I find another lover?
I hurried, hungry, from the Trojan Wars

only to find it padlocked, and no other
to call me Sugar when I'm in the mood.
The final Yum Yum Shoppe has closed its doors.

I'd come to warn you, shopkeep: anything
concerning horses will be marveled at.
I hurried, hungry, in my torn velour,

hauled ass to tell you anything at all
you haven't, in the long haul, understood.
The final Yum Yum Shoppe has closed its doors:

our combat's caused most businesses to fold,
the Swill&Swing I'd kick my heels up at
burned down last March. I hurried, harried, home

toward what I knew as constant. Nothing was.
No mallomars for Horst and Little Inga.
Each warmth recedes. All doors, by nature, close.
Sexy like thieves, we rush from war to war.

She was like a headless Mary,
but with a head.

I wanted to curl up
behind my stove like a small mammal,

but we were outdoors.
Clouds were shifting.

I couldn't remember
the country my duplex was in.

Later that day, we were walking
on stuff that some trees left behind,

she in her green antebellum chemise,
I in my half-cocked felt hat,

past the abandoned nail salon,
the boarded-up Etruscan discotheque.

I felt compelled to inform her
of all the things she was thinking,

so I reached my good hand
toward the Budweiser blimp overhead

and said, that's one hell
of a blimp overhead.

She asked me whether
she could cling to me

on the Impaler,
no, the Tilt-a-Whirl,

at the next Church
of Wounded Jesus carnival.

I wanted to live for
an infinite while

on the outskirts of Troy
at the dawnbreak of siege,

where I would conduct
reenactments

of meeting her
in my spare time.

The Rainy Season

Her penicillined me. Her found a shirt
moths hadn't ravaged; swaddled me in said
apparel. Said, *Go west, young man. Here's looking*

at you, kid, her said, and *Remember the Maine.*
Her stenciled me a mouth, as I had none
to speak of, and affixed it to my face,

a tad off-center. Pressed her lips against.
I was a sniffling, lanky aggregate.
Her served my body absinthe, for the pain.

Her fashioned me an astrolabe, sewed flags
for me to wave at her from far away.
I called her History (her had no name).

I didn't love her, so I said I did,
and just about fell over from those words,
the guilt thereof, then gestured to my groin.

Outside, the rain did awful things to trees.
The television called for years of rain,
with drought to follow. *You will never stroll,*

History muttered, as her stroked my neck,
regardless of intent, through the same door,
with your umbrella twice, toward the same world

into the same predicament and weather.

Cancer Is a Disease of Animals

When she said she would rather cut
what was intimate out of her, out of her skin,
out of the frame she was in, cut it out,

her involvement with him, like a tumor,
when she said she would rather kill,
if not for shame, herself, than stay beside,

through the continuance on one damp sheet
of one more night, him, that she'd rather die
than lay her shopworn body next to his again,

when she said, *it's no use, we're like having a cancer
distend in and through me*, he wanted to say,
as he cut, for propriety's sake, himself off

from the saying of it, *it's a beautiful thing*,
and she, not having heard him, did not ask,
why must you mumble so, which thing, and he,

she not having had asked him, could not reply, *cancer,
I find cancer beautiful, were I to choose
a terminal illness to be, I would cancer,*

*not cystic fibrosis, not me, psoriatic arthritis,
would cancer and not beriberi what have you,
had I some say in it.* He would have liked

to mean by what he could not find the breath inside
the fog-and-wetness of his lungs enough to say,
the frenzy of it, cancer's sprawl and raw,

*the spring of thing from nothing, the tense bloom
of the imperative of* give *like moss on wall,
forsythia on snow, like wall on ivy.*

He would have liked *give up* to lunge at her,
give in to push, onto a pillow, back her face,
to pull *give give* into his throat her breath,

to rent her body for an endlessness,
to cover her and swell and hold and say,
to whisper *hi there* under her left breast,

to fog-and-wetness her and say and hold,
to mean by what he could not find the breath inside,
to say and say until all matter ceased.

1

I would for you turn down the thermostat

Turn off the fire in the corridor

The fire licking at your comforter

The Punic Wars on your front lawn if my remote

Control had batteries in it I'd turn you on

Keeping you on for weeks like overhead

Lights in a house whose occupants have left

For holiday in the Maldives

If I had hands I would for you take off

Fatigues I've worn since Breath enlisted me

Expose the barrel chest and shrapnel wounds

Concealed by said fatigues if I had hands

If I had knees I'd be on one of them

Kneeling like fog kneels in an alleyway

Right now on the uneven floor your shadow

Is occupying (falling through) I have

No knees for you no barrel chest nothing to pass

For hands only a voice that won't turn off

Despite the switches flipped the trigger pulled

2

Has one of us taken the other of us for a ride?
Has one of us mistaken the other of us for a ride
at the State Fair? Have we been fair to each other
in our affairs with the candy shop girl,

the small arms manufacturer? Crisscrossed the carpet
bombed Empire together, petting the elegant
children that maundered the smoldering parking lots.
Rode a mechanical bull. Panted softly.

*Nothing that has ever happened should
be regarded as lost*, wrote Walter Benjamin,
who overdosed on morphine in the Pyrenees,
locking his final thoughts in a valise

his friends misplaced. The local gravediggers
misplaced his body at the cemetery.
As soon as something happens, it is lost:
the hillock of a shoulderblade your hand

is passing over, the Etruscan boy who shouts
"I'll never not adore you" in his long-lost
native alphabet, our amorous, coy, canorous
ways of diverting time. Has one of us

outloved the other yet? Has one of us refused
acknowledging having outloved the other yet?
As soon as something happens, it is lost.
Nobody knows where Benjamin is buried.

3

Q: Are you sick with self-pity?
At the masked ball, no one noticed me.

Q: Were you wearing a mask?
I have worn many things I had thought would conceal me.

Q: Will you unlace my too-tight whalebone corset?
It sure can't be easy to breathe with it on.

Q: Will you unlace my too-tight whalebone corset?
*To the masked ball, I wore gabardine slacks. It wasn't easy to breathe
    with them on.*

Q: May I offer you thimbles, a sewing machine, a cushion to bury
   your face in?
*At the Museum of Body Parts, I saw the earlobe (pierced) of a small
   girl, detached from her, in a glass jar. This piercing scared me.*

Q: What have you mastered?
They gave me high marks for Industrial Arts, Elocution.

Q: What do you think you've forgotten?
The one thing I do is remember.

Q: What do you know you've forgotten?
Composure. The taste of persimmon. To turn off the overhead light.

Q: Where do you grieve?
I have crawlspaces hidden inside me.

Q: Will you unlace my too-tight whalebone corset?
*O, for a cushion to bury my face in. O, for your hand to extinguish the
   light.*

TWO

There comes the point
in every story
when I panic,

there comes this panic,
I catch myself clutching
a wrench at a Wal-Mart,

a wren in a field,
clutching a wrist
near a radio tower,

or someone's key
I had not been aware of,
turning the knob

of a make-believe door.
Body the contour
of jazz in a speakeasy,

body the texture
of gasps in a gangway,
why I keep letting

you down is beyond me.
I've taken pains.
Practiced synchronized breathing.

Counted past ten.
Talked with zeal about things.
Even summoned the nerve

to look fetching in amber.
But can't get past
that which rattles inside me.

Try to think back:
was I going
to flash you or juggle.

Or was there a story
I needed to tell you.
Was it important.

Could it have swayed you.
I meant to give objects
totemic significance,

refer to a childhood,
invoke certain towns.
And would I have broken

one heart or another.
It was the story of my life,
it would have started

with the note la,
then a couple of llamas.
Sometimes, a window fan

would, in it, pass for an eye.
Trust me,
it would have been riveting.

Outside, the stink of gas
seeped by vermicular streets.
Baku is a city steeped

in gas. The black morass
of the Caspian Sea has no fish.
The natives thrive on gas.
They know no other smell.

For reasons beyond my control,
I eat potatoes and wear
a bib in Azerbaijan,

where I wasn't born,
where the muezzins will not
spread word of my death.
And the potatoes are rough

and cold. Cold, the hands
of our hostess who prods
my mouth with a long fork.

Eat! Eat! She pleads. I eat.
The hostess serves us tea
in orange bowls. We sip.
I spill some on my lap.

Is there a zoo, I ask,
because I want to ask
the right question.

Of course, she sighs, we have
a zoo, but the only
animal left is a wolf
with no skin on one side.

The Age of Reason

The architecture and the tide were mine
to hold dominion over, and I tried

to reassure, for what it's worth, the poor.
I minted coins. I coined essential phrases.

I said, *Let there be food*, and no one starved.
Made sure the banquets had more shrimp than last year.

Parades were held. I listened to applause,
commissioned ziggurats to please the pious,

and drowned the feral cats, for what it's worth.
For what it's worth, I bayoneted the last hecklers.

Mailed letters of condolence to the towns
the hecklers used, for what it's worth, to kiss

their mothers in. Their mothers answered me
in girlish scrawl on the backsides of postcards.

Writing, *It is lonely in the Quonset hut,*
but thank you for the solar power plant,

God bless you for the ice rink at the mall,
the Monroe Doctrine, and the Ferris Wheel.

Writing, *Sorrow I'm filled with for what my firstborn . . .*
I raised, for what it's worth, the mothers' pensions.

Box-stepped all night with emissaries' wives
beneath the chandeliers of the State Ballroom,

played checkers with my neighbor to the north,
and shot at butterflies through open windows.

The Ordered Mind in the Disordered House

The what is what the how will never know.
The clock is here. And elsewhere, there are clocks.

A creaking always is at some o'clock.
It steadies—clockwork—after some o'clock.

The clocks are faster now. The air smells. Well.
Now, dashing swattings at some flying thing.

The well not that where all the water was.
The flying thing one wishes to have seen.

A mandate to believe. What else with wings.
At some o'clock, the body tends to heal.

Has suffered through. All the assessments of.
There is a number here. Can't find the phone.

Accomplish seldom, yet do not detract.
The what is what the how will never know.

And twigs. And months. And moths. Now are. Then then.
What carpet stains. What abscesses. What tastes.

Stop being, but leave something of the once.
The leaving of no course but to obsess.

Books travel from that nightstand to this floor.
And ribbons smattered here, the ash and spit.

If plans are followed through, one might distract.
What lonesome warmth. What comfortable warmth.

One rotten everything. One washed parquet.
One limb that feels as foreign as your limb.

The sounds one takes for breathing. The two ears.
The hisses of. The of. The orders for.

Is this for me. Why I do not believe.
The orders of. The hisses for. The for.

The what is what the how will never know.
Outside, large objects move. Or so who says.

Is this for me. I manage. I believe.
One more enormous door. And faster clocks.

There are a couple somethings always on.
In the long meantime, that and why not those.

In the long meantime, tell them as they seem.
These so many not goods being told.

Do not endeavor
to snapshot the locals.

Do not trust anything
that could snap shut.

Try to pass quickly
through slipshod locales.

Do not give alms.
Make no eye contact.

Do not confuse
yourself with your reflection,

this span of ruins with a system,
this inn with a place to come back to.

Rein in the impulse to build
a new city from these scattered twigs.

Do not poke around in the abandoned
houses of the damaged village.

Do not get curious
about shiny metal in the grass.

Do not plant kisses
on the blind accordionist.

Leave the mermaid alone,
it is not meant to be.

You will cause offense.
You will not hear the knob turn.

You will wake to find stones in your mouth
and a lake in each eye.

Do not ring the concierge.
Do not search for the consulate.

Regard every centimeter
of ground as suspicious.

Trains are essentially useless.
The timetable lies.

Each day you are bound
to lose something.

*Each day you are bound
to lose something.*

Do not meander too far
from a given road's shoulder.

Owning a car does not give
you the clearance to drive.

I chose to disregard
the Plague of Thebes,
the crowd of bees, the shadow
boxing tournament.

Forgot what terror meant.
Drank Coca-Cola
in flagrant violation of the law,
and glanced at stones,

went on about my business.
But, having thumbed
through my phrasebook and found
the terms *paramour, loss*

of composure, and *curtsey,*
I made the effort to love some
not-me like a one-legged man
loves his one leg.

I applied much mascara
in anticipation, affected
the postures and faces
prescribed by my *Rough Guide.*

How is it I figured
time for a step forward?
I went to a bar
and then one more bar

and then I went home,
and he who I thought
would not follow me,
followed me.

Gold Rush

A naked hitchhiker. Three scarecrows.
A burning shrub near Ashtabula.
A whale of a truck wreck. A sparrow

with only one wing. Forty rainfalls,
an empty Best Western and fifty
of us on a bus, some with reasons,

the scent of departure escaping
through yesterday's pores, while my seatmate
goes on about lushness, the lushness

to come. There are mounds. There is desert;
hey big guy you know if it's Tuesday?
One toddler yelps curses. Is silenced.

Our driver does not speak my language.
Each window has yielded to Wednesday.
Hey big guy when will it be Tuesday?

My seatmate is gone. Men get hammered.
They poke at a woman in labor.
I try to remember. *Hey tiny*

so what do you know about lushness?
I wash off my hands at each rest stop.
My family smiles in my nightmares.

The smokestacks we pass keep recurring.
The billboards we pass lead to famine.
The hammered ones leave in the Valley.

Hey big guy can I be your seatmate?

1

I've, for one, had it
to here with the Food Channel,
it's like they're always cooking
a duck or something,
carving a duck's carcass
or whatever.
Whaddaya say,
just one road trip together,
up the Menominee,
through the Ardennes?
We will sit in a rowboat.
Will watch barges pass us.
The moon, I mean,
the sun is beautiful,
settling down over
what stays nearby,
while someone not here
starts intoning *Earth Angel*
and we spot the moon
through dense trees like a lost
giant's flashlight.

2

The Banishment
Capital of the World,
you know, where they've
sent all the witches,
the two-headed oxen,
boys who insist
they are mermaids,
the bowlegged gymnasts,
is oft confused
with Elkhart, Indiana,

the Band Instrument
Capital of the World,
and in certain fog
with Sheboygan.
Each after all
has a barber
named Felix
and on occasion
a lunar eclipse,
half a hill
strewn with marigolds.

The poem was a razorblade, glinting and modern.
An archaeologist caught sight of it under the fallen

midsection of a Doric column in the buried
Albanian walled city of Butrint. He didn't mean

to cut, but cut, his knuckle on its edge. The poem
was a two-story house on Burlap Street

in a forgotten segment of Chicago.
The poem was the path of the syringe

into the punctured vein, the spine propped up against
the house's wainscoting. The snow that slipped

onto the house's mailbox and the tree lawn
was not the poem, but a seasonal disorder

the snowblowers and calendar would cure.
Nor was the poem the lie the lover told

in the last letter to arrive that winter.
The poem was the mail that failed to bear

sufficient postage, having spent the last
ten years of its existence in a drawer.

Bulgaria's covered in roses, the dead
letter intended to say to a lover.

The poem was a Bulgarian who loitered
in a Bulgarian pasture, blushing from

the thousands of roses paving it.
The poem was the Bulgarian's bad posture.

The poem was his hair. I watched it turn
from black to silver in the time it took

for the chill Balkan sunlight to recede
into the ether. The poem was the ether

rag I would sink my lips and nostrils in
to make myself absent, feel better.

Were you to glue electrodes to its skull,
forcefeed it serum, tamper with its body,

the poem would disappoint or disappear.
The poem was untrustworthy, a matter

too slippery to not, too soon, let go of.
In its tiara and the décolletage

holding in place the muscles of its chest,
the poem could be mistaken for you, reader.

Your eyes are not glass eyes, but might as well . . .
The poem didn't know of its severe

astigmatism, its desperate need to tamper
with the official record of the past.

The poem was the past that failed to happen,
the panic in God's voice each time he used it,

the doubting tone the Hebrew scribes were frightened
to indicate to those who hadn't heard him.

The poem was not God's voice, but the long sequence
of rapid breaths the sky took prior to opening

over Butrint and Burlap Street each morning.

1

Some of the news was political.
Streetlamps lost bright when they passed me.
Fitting my self in my body,
I would tear seams.

I thought the woman I came from
spent nighttimes with lizards and nightshade.
I asked whether God was around me.
She wouldn't say.

2

There was a blizzard
I almost remember.

(There was a thought and
I almost remember).

Somebody taught complex fractions.
Somebody froze in our yard.

Each morning I opened the door and descended—
how lovely, I think, the pale sidewalks,

ice limbing across them, the dawdling
murders of birds.

3

I'd walk and, sometimes, saunter
away from that rhombus which keeps me,

through figures and frames which deny me,
to stand under broken up wind,

and the birds did not skirl, and two jet trails
(each one with its vacuum of erstwhiles)

(and what is it not to be human)
(and is it a difference or anything)

(I say and sometimes mean)
slashed past each other in a white cross.

4

. . . they had an assembly before his enrollment . . .
. . . the motive was warning (or were they just frightened) . . .
. . . he was covered in cloth . . .

. . . there were fires . . .
         . . . were slits for consuming and seeing. . . .

. . . each morning his mother would change it . . .
         . . . the principal mouthed the word *tactful* . . .

. . . how did the camera lens react . . .
         . . . we all walked past him . . .

. . . I had to hold onto my wrist, I had to keep it from . . .
         . . . extending toward the what, toward where the skin
should be . . .

         . . . and how one approaches . . .
. . . dilemmas like grieving. . . .

I may be redundancy's concubine, asking the light for more light.

5

Heights on account of what loiters alongside
Heights on account of how what can leave where

Water it came before everything it is not leaving
Fire its charrings in corners each remnant of breath

Openness ample and grand and not mortal yet in its cherubic decor
Every enclosure each mobbing of room each low ceiling

42

Or sundry people the stirs the weird slurrings of people
Or seeing one after one after one and then all

Being buried alive hearing gravel in slippage
Or turning bald or incontinent near only stones

6

Even some grim with a chimney with smoke from it
Even a wall with a window which prints on it

Even a teapot the teapot had tea in it
Even a novel the novel had breath in it

Even a wall just one wall just one face on it
Even a smoke and the lovers made love to it

Even a floorboard the floorboard had tea on it
Even a face while some smoke puddled eyes in it

Even a chimney the squirrels lacking breath in it
Even a print of a palm with no arm to it

Even a chimney and pages rest under it
Even a puddle what chimneys strain up through it

7

never the darkening
but the white vastness

the unremitting of climate
the sprawling of wings

how one keeps up
this ambiguous thrashing

this what alongside
a firm disremembering

and what to cling to
save fragments of language

cadaverous
in their repetitive soft

8

Which dancing fool Which lake's effect Which chosen people

Which ice cream headache Which *beau fleuve* Which love's canal

Which velcro shoes Which secret sauce Which Erie county

Which metal rise Which skillful aging Which last rites

Which brand of forty Which big falls Which coefficient

Which blouse concealing what

Which weeds remain

9

Not pointing at objects,
not swallowing insects, I
rode someone's giant wheel
over a tightrope and after,
and although the sky stayed unclean
with black holes and lost eyes
I was bad at not seeing,
no part of my person was thinking,
no part of me cheering me on.

I feigned I was the only one,
at least in Buffalo.

It was another month.
The saddest thing.

THREE

When I Was Pol Pot

While the uncommon
music fogged past smiles,

I was wish-slender,
mango-round and flawed,

perfect and breathing
communal soup-warm,

and not wanting to
lie, while stray casings

and slight trunks of trees
lined each avenue

in this not common
singsong of Phnom Penh,

where I liked cream-filled
sweets, and found myself

in glass, face gracing
each vitrine, and lay

through dreams of flying,
and stayed scared, while this

common unmusic
whined, of everything

I did not know, and
sanctioned more than one

fire, mosquito,
unwinding, and grave.

Today, on the Obituary Channel

Fell asleep in his Jeep heading out of Canarsie
Tangoed onto a land mine in Hazard Kentucky
In Hollywood slowly of undisclosed causes
Suddenly during a terminal illness
A suicide following open heart surgery
On the family farm in the clutch of a mistress
By lethal injection while singing
The Battle Hymn of the Republic missing
And still presumed to have invented solitaire
The self-proclaimed Sultan of Cockfighting
Heir to the throne of Qatar
Later an interview with his betrothed
Now stay tuned for a tour of the Providence morgue
Live from the cave where he long ago painted
Live from the world where he chipped his first tooth
Is survived by his mother

Restraint

After my mother dies
on some near evening,

I must do everything
mourners do: scream,

cut up my hair, slash her shoes,
let our neighbors unlearn us.

I must pass time.
I must pass lots of time

in the commodious white
of the bed which conceived of me.

I have to memorize Ruth
and recite her,

backwards, to haphazard Hebrews.
I must learn Hebrew

and worship some gods.
I must buy slaughterhouse futures.

I must watch flies fly into beards.
I must believe

in my future and stay
fetal for days, self-importantly.

I must believe in Thermopylae,
the Defenestration of Prague.

I must read more about the life
of Rutherford B. Hayes.

I must carol, *meiosis, mitosis,*
and not let my eyes glaze.

I must divide complex fractions
until I grow weary.

I must devise
games to make myself wary.

I must run bare
through the crowded gymnasium

with a geranium jammed
into the crook of each ear.

I must stum wine.
I must stum lots of wine.

I must pass lots of time.
I must pass time.

I must not drag
my ill skin to the hearse,

worn from the need
to make love

to her truant, calm body.

We Require an Assertion of Value, We Are Frightened

1

Before we who survived came to appreciate
cellophane and the fandango,
slot machines, lisping, and overtures,
walking and white,
before we started questioning
insistence on the specificity of digits,
before we, too, demanded specificity
and bought a scarf
because some neck displeased us,
before we dressed ourselves,
when others dressed us—
they fed us things we fail to talk about—
we ran around in laps. We called it playing.
We stood on coals for hours. We called it playing.
We played with rough and sharp.
When parents let us,
when parents reached for wine and did not pry,
we knelt. We reverenced.
We started plotting
on our big hill of thought a cross of bone.

2

Ya-hey and la and la.
Tell me: who stopped it?
Who stole the small train, the big slinky,
the ermine stole imagined from a towel?
The puzzle, it couldn't be solved.
Where is the jungle? The Korean orphan?
Where did three goldfish go? That game is lost.
That game not here, those here for now now have
to find the murderer, the path
to bed and heretofore. The urge
to believe in the blood that doesn't exist

cannot cure or be purchased.
Are you the murderer? Is who the slink?
Where did I hide the block, the pricking
pins, the oval toy, my head, the deaf
boy I beat up, the embraces,
the wine the grown-ups left, the friend
I made from coat hangers? What did we keep?

The Babel Hyatt Regency stays vacant
except for us and many phones not sounding.
We are alone. There is an eye not winking.
We are alone and do not want to know
what time it is. And do not want to say
too much. And do not want to touch
too much and do.

3

Imagine our relief, our disappointment,
when someone told us the grenade
we had discovered, the grenade
we took delight in kicking to each other,
was just a clump of night or else some earth
or just a heart or else
some lesser organ.

My Mayakovsky

I walk through Moscow in my yellow shirt.
I stagger in my sallow shirt through dusky Moscow,
brick lilies blossoming the length of its grey parkways.
I rest a pistol on my temple. Nothing happens.
I, in my scandalous yellow, have traversed
the length of grey, dirt-lovely Moscow, past the odors
of rifle-fire and fresh bread, slamming my fist
against the lacquer of my chamber's red armoire
until my knuckles bleed. With my red hand, I trace
the many letters of my name over my chest.
My knuckles blister as I gently rest,
on my armoire, my pistol, storing my luck
in one of its six chambers, but which one?
My lifetime, darling, stay with me forever.
Dear lifetime, I can't bear you any longer.
I telegram inferior poets the good news
of their departure and my repertoire, then skid
past mists of mink and nimbuses in squirrel
over the glacial streets of wintry Moscow.
Lifetime the length of a papercut. Of a parade
of soldiers through the snow. Length of my chamber
in the housing tower. Length of my Soviet Union, of a song
that can't remember how to end itself. I rest
the trigger on my frontmost teeth; the barrel
feels cold against the barrel of my throat.
You bound and gagged me, passionate, cold lover.
Lifetime the brevity of our encounter.
Down with your love, I wrote in each boudoir.
Down with your art, I wired the Hermitage.
I told the officer, *Down with your social order*.
Down with your worshiping, I whispered to my mother.
Down with my faith in you, Creator, who dismembers
and sews me back together every hour.
I telegram inferior poets to inquire
why readers love and understand them better.

Down with your hair, Maria.
Down with your hair, Lily Brik.
I hide my shirt in a wool suit and march
my polished boots through Moscow, brandishing
my heart's four chambers, skewered, on a rapier.
I rest a pistol on my temple. Fire.

Crime Spree

Drug it, rob it, just deposit
what you will of one lean body,
folded over like fresh linen

near some lindens, far from traffic.
Every season in our shtetl
it gets tougher to make do with:

buy the beggar girl a flower.
Steal the beggar girl two flowers
from the only kiosk open.

In the abandoned mausoleum,
lend her your pullover,
lie that you want her.

Call her Tatiana, Keeper of the Bears.
Tell her she's destined to sleep
with a paw on each shoulder.

Were there a chance her arms
would keep you warm,
she'd sell you

her embrace for fifty kopecks.
Go on. There is a chance
you'll keep her warm.

The Bouvet Øya Lighthouse Keeper Speaks After Protracted Silence

The remotest island in the world is Bouvet Øya, in the South Atlantic. . . . This uninhabited Norwegian dependency is about 1,050 miles from the nearest land—the uninhabited Queen Maud Land coast of eastern Antarctica.
—1992 Guinness Book of World Records

I'm only here to hold back
crashings of seal against rock,

to thwart each irregular mooring
of lifeboat. On this ice-damp,

I comb for lichen, smell
burnt branch where there is none.

Unadoptable bone-hardy truancy: I
know what the odds are. Deposit

of hillock on water, I lack
other children. Lost off-ramp in Jersey,

I've left behind my spring dress,
my big pocket of stuff.

Each night, I name each step,
look out on what will stay,

hear blowing. Hold me back
from loss, foster parent of cold.

I can no longer tell
a lilac from world's wane.

Queen Maud Land's weather shifts
over what lights and breathing.

My supplies are gone.
I surrender this.

The Refraction

Our memory of *then* is an old mare
caught in a flood, is a flood washing
the weathered things past us. This water
whirls by with impatience like a first

fall, a first fright, through a thicket.
This thicket, which clears out the figures
who stood and the phrases we took to
be ravishing, that is the memory.

There is no voice here, no breath
breaching the denseness of everything
here in this comatose, this all-encompassing
where our machetes have failed us,

where, in knurled patterns, some yesterdays
sweep over branches like tentative
shadows of clouds. And that *then*
in our memory is this continual

prayer for sound.

Life with García Márquez on Long Island

Even when burying
friends, we were happy.

Even when dancing on tiptoe
with knives past the widescreen TV.

World undone, speak to me
please of that nuanced

snarl of Ronkonkoma
where someone sleepy

once touched you and dropped
from the wind of his sleeve

a tornado of objects,
each glistening

prior to losing itself
in the decay of your yard.

Evenings we spend
still persuading each other

there is a branch
weighing down on one skylight

and not a strange man
                    with extravagant wings.

The Death of Elegy

Reluctant, I must onward, dearest wantword, fairest ragebird:
I can no longer in the throatscratched marshland,
nor do I find myself capable in the Cathedral of Learning,

or any(for that matter)where in Pittsburgh.

Have lugged too many bodies through its freightyards
in my translucent slip. In my gauche veil, I thought
I'd steel myself against despair, did not accomplish.

The moon is black tonight, as if there is none.

The moon tonight is either black, or stolen,
and I do not possess the wherewithal
to up-and-down, in search for it, on the funiculars.

What I've become. An overcoat with hands,

hands I would fail to feel if it were colder.
The Line of Demarcation has been drawn.
How to keep mourning, missing, anyone,

with Johnstown flooded, Carthage sacked, Rome sacked,

the Parthenon in ruins, you gone, Pittsburgh a ghost
that silhouettes, when clouds are scarce, the marshland.
Try keeping up, these days, with all that's gone.

Each gust of wind collapses through my fingers.

FOUR

Professional Extra

Because I could spend twenty takes on a Ferris wheel.
On account of my jaundice. My thyroid condition.

I had a nice ass and the requisite body weight.
Knew how to walk through a door unobtrusively,

as if for the last time, but still, unobtrusively.
Could pass for whomever was passing through Fresno,

or carry umbrellas so as to conceal
any trace of a person conspiring beneath them.

Director said, *Man on the edge of a platform*
with a bouquet of nasturtiums and checking

his pocketwatch, fidgeting, like there is someone
he knows won't arrive on the Eastbound sleeper.

First, I am skiing alongside the villain
in *Ski Party Four*: villain says to me, *Gus,*

or whatever they call you, move over, you're standing
too much between me and the camera you're blocking.

Later, I'm cast as a stiff in a coffin.
The reason they cut me: I can't keep from trembling.

Whenever they call me, I find myself trembling.
Another occasion: I die with my boots on,

impaled on a pool cue. Once, die with no face on.
Director said, *No, you're a serial killer.*

You're a professional flasher. A wallflower.
The villain from *Ski Party Four* plays Robespierre

in the new costume drama *Reign of Terror,*
and I have been placed on an as-needed basis:

time will decide if history will have me.
The heart is a construct I cobble together

from outtake to outtake. It runs in the family.
For me, the sweet smell of periphery. Timid

and weird in my clothes, I do everything
poorly, but with great affection. I merge

with the traffic of every encounter, take care
not to exhibit too much character, lose sight

of being watched. To the premiere, I wear
whatever I had on the day before.

The Ferris wheels are suddenly, and everywhere.

All the Greatest Stories Ever Told

Once ran a carnival
just east of Onset—

after the fire,
he was out of monkeys.

Once laughed so hard
he fell out of a train.

Once laughed so hard
he thought his face would shatter.

The figurines Once used
to shudder near

began to pass
for doubles of his mother.

His mother's thick fingerbones
squeezing his own.

The spondee *Black Night*
whispered into his body.

World hasn't had
a lover more demure.

Locked the knives in a drawer.
Only seldom threw vases.

Said, can you take me
to your bat cave, baby.

Said, can you help
unwrap this lollipop for me.

Word of his fistfight
with one tipsy roustabout

reached Marblehead,
or so he liked to fancy.

Mercy have mercy et cetera,
Once did not say

on the night he broke down
in the glowing casino.

The Frustrated Vaudevillian

How I miss Lisbon,
where I've never been.
It is autumn again,
it has always been autumn.

I scar my face
with a mishandled razor.
I clean each ear
to let music in.

My voice is scarred
by voices better than.
I have lost track of acts.
Here is a terror

and there, the distances
I have forgotten
of fancied pseudonyms
and what I think.

So many dishes wait . . .

A wealth of trinkets . . .

I search remains of rooms for pie and laudanum . . .

I draw the curtains tight.
I yawn all night.
I try to kiss what
greets me in the mirror.

Kwashiorkor

After a lifetime, I still
search each wrong wall for the lightswitch.

Haven't we met, I demand
of the washcloth, I ask of the escort.

Do I recall me, the one who has not
lent his name to a vineyard.

After a lifetime, I stall
at the crest of a sentence.

What did I do, I left fingerprints.
What did I do, I climbed rocks.

How swell it would be if I only
had faith in the Theory of Everything,

sashayed down the mauve promenade
in my fishnet sarong.

Joy to the world then, but wait,
have I done the cryptography.

Can, in the scheme of things, *y*
equal every *not x*.

After a lifetime, I straddle
the sidelines of pictureframes.

And how unwieldy, my cellophane caul.
And how forbidding, this light fixture.

What did we do, we were going to say.
What did we do, we made mention.

What did we do, we brushed dark with our teeth
at some beachhouse near Cape Disappointment,

and what is the climate like in not this body.
Is that an awning there within the scaffolding.

Tell me, sweet pal, if the water is boiling,
how is it you navigate toward every ending,

your lips in a grin, your arms opened wide,
holding neither a wand nor a fire extinguisher.

Disorder, but which one? I fall, back first,
against the chests of strangers I have paid
not to fall backwards from my torso's weight.
Their shorthand distillations of what's wrong
fold seamlessly into my wallet's folds.
The Paxil and the Klonopin are one.
The Effexor lies down with the lamb.
After each devastation, I'm alone,
the wallpaper as handsome where I am
as in my childhood, curling at the edges
like paperbacks inhabited too long.
After each devastation, a parade
holds itself in my honor: the sirens,
the garters, the left-behind lover,
and, salvaged from the previous parade,
half in Cyrillic, half illegible, a banner.
Was I, before this devastation, holding
my breath in your mouth, your bone wristwatch
clasped in the restraint of my hand? I was busy
discussing apostasy, Joey Ramone, the preserved
lock of Milton's red hair in a foreign museum,
the Nasdaq, the naughty volcanoes inside us.
Distracting myself with your tenuous body
I told you belonged in a foreign museum.
Disorder, but which one? The medication
arrives with new side effects and a decoder
ring for the children. I ring for the doctor
and threaten to leave her. I swallow my Buspar,
feel dizzy all over. They wilt while I plant them,
my devious flowers. The worst gardener ever,
on Ritalin, I can stay moving for hours
and weeks. On Celexa, I've learned to feel nothing.
I ring for the doctor. I threaten to love her.
She offers me soup from a Styrofoam casket.
We holiday beside the tension wires,

cooing *I Wanna Be Sedated* to each other.
She slips me Xanax, grants me her brassiere
to rest over my eyes until they shutter.
Disorder, but which one? The patent leather
restraints keep me flat but have not made me better
at solving—for her—the quadratic equation
where we stand for exes. She threatens to fuck me,
a terrible doctor. She tells me she's only
a woman pretending she knows what the cure is
for everything wrong. I take steps to believe her.
Pacing her heelprints past me and away,
she faults the pills for crazy, faults the dose
and barometric pressure, faults my skill
at leaving my prescriptions unfulfilled
for crazy. *The Disordered One*, my calm-
in-her-confusion doctor takes to calling me.
Napoleon Blown-Apart, she takes (mistake)
to heckling me each time I pace the length
of the tricorner bedroom, muttering
about the friends misplaced at Austerlitz,
Fallujah, and the Somme. This mind conflates
visions of scuffles that could never have,
without the drugs, occurred the way the drugs
insist they did. After the devastation, hearing
the distant cry of sirens, we applaud.
If the parade won't save us, nothing will.

We have diabetes (and hypoglycemia)

Heart murmurs (yeast

Where it doesn't belong)

(This is the human condition) Samantha

Has rickets (she hears each bone soften)

She swears to her doctor (he fails to believe her)

He's losing his patients (there's talk of malpractice)

He's not a bad doctor his patience is fading

Rosario (whose dog has hip dysplasia)

Had Hepatitis B got over it

Calls to explain she is dying from lupus

She's had it since grade school but no one had told her

On her end of the line there are silences (static)

She could be calling from (Ecuador) Sparta

She is downstairs (she was setting the table

For one when the phone rang with news from the clinic)

We have diabetes and hypoglycemia

We're sick with desire (the human condition)

Cough syrup (children) a bladder infection

A touch of bursitis (we're tired of our bodies)

We're frightened we reach for inhalers (have children

We name with impatience in hospital hallways)

Our children speak up they insist they are suffering

From beautiful nouns (impetigo the measles

Blepharospasm stage fright) Arshile gets the shakes

Every morning while towering over his pancake

We can't have the sugar the sugar will save us

The city's fenced off every sound is contagious

Our fibromyalgia our chronic nostalgia

(There's talk of a cure which has not been approved yet

We tell one another believing each phoneme)

How we are conditioned to fend for each other

To kiss the warm forehead of somebody's fever

To clasp the cold hand of a body that's left us

How we are conditioned to get ourselves over

Ourselves to get over another's departure

(Rosario's funeral falls on a Tuesday)

Notice us we're

Getting younger and younger

The cots are cold and damp. All patients dream
of being diagnosed. Those without tongues
complain the least. Nurse Agnes comes each dawn
to change the sheets: all patients dream of her
on crutches in her ironed uniform.

While emptying our bedpans one by one,
she'll flash her bra strap if we ask real nice,
croon *Camp Town Races* and the *Thong Song.*
When she departs, for want of games, we jot
equations down on one another's casts,

call one another Sweetheart. What we dream
we can remember only in our sleep.
This plagues us like our plagues plague what is left
of what our bodies were. Our bodies were
what other bodies dreamt about. At least,

on lunch breaks at the plant, on promenades
past the arcade at night, in the soft beds
we used to occupy, they would confess
that when they slept alone, they couldn't help
but see us in the tunnels of their sleep,

that seeing us in dreams did not suffice.
We fiddle with the bracelets on our wrists:
soon, after hours, the orderly will come,
the one whose name we've never learned to say
will shuffle through our antiseptic dusk,

take note of each of us with his pale eyes.

Pompeii

I stick a coin over each socket.
Is there a wall to contain every body?
Where is the famous escape artist hiding?

Somebody stitched him onto a mountain.
I stitch a smile onto each canvas.
I drink the vacuum of a dry fountain.

What were you scared of, a mountain on fire

Says the red wall, says the escapist to the wall,
the stolen camera says. A trip can sew
a palm into a palm, say the blind vendors,

a knee into pavement, echoes the archway,
a view into an archway, an escape artist
into a mountain, hands over a face.

I took a mountain of a blue picture

Somebody trapped it under an archway.
I also was taken by how all kept standing.
And I took a picture of my being taken,

and of a white face in a plastic container,
white hands closing in--every icon needs framing.
How much there is to want. Too much to frame.

There were other hands, I made efforts to see them

for mine, this stone post for my home, this disabled
escape artist for one more someone to follow.
This is the mountain his hands are chained to.

Who gave you this fire you frame your face with,
I ask of no one. I refuse to want.
I sheathe each blade. I search for knives and water.

What were you thinking, a mountain on fire

I do not think, says the wall while collapsing.

I am in love, says the man to his casket.
Whom can I own? asks the somnolent master.

Whom can I love? I get by.

Certain Things

are awkward, they
will not withstand such trespasses.

In the Wyoming of each day,
the square in which

each circle burns, they fidget much,
move little, pick at, pick.

Conditions vary. Furnishings
remain. Have you succeeded yet

in setting the table, the tone,
the example, the record straight?

You have surrendered:
you have persevered,

watching the tumbleweed
race itself down the main drag

past the locked storefronts
and acres of weather.

Why must you stumble over
the third buttonhole

with all this panic
fastened to your face?

You joined in the search
for a cat in the water, you tipped

the paramedic and played
Let's Misbehave for the killer,

you clung to the park sculpture, mouthing
please go away and *I need.*

Harpsichords slide
off one balcony. While the chalk outlines ascend,

does it distress you to know
that tonight might get breezier, colder?

As though in Bulgaria, shake your head no,
meaning yes, it is always like this.

Let me mistake your smile
for happiness, your restlessness for sleep,

your bones for offerings, you for
a god, myself for you. Let me

and other aborigines, if that
is what some history or child will say we are,

fragilities of here, your shadow's wants,
draw close and whisper lies into your ear.

Go hunt that small of marble, huge of earth, that thing
you haven't seen in ages or before,

that ease of speech, that wish you owned, the nameless one.
There are too many passages to love.

Joseph Cornell, with Box

World harbors much I'd like to fit inside
that the parameters preclude me from.

I'm the desire to have had a say.
I'm the desire to be left alone

amid brochures for Europe's best hotels
behind a locked door on Utopia Parkway,

where Brother, crippled, rides his chariot,
where Mother's all dressed up and going nowhere.

Together, *sotto voce*, we count hours,
fuss over newsprint, water down the wine.

When I was shorter, we were all divine.
When I was shorter, I was infinite

and felt less fear of being understood.
I am the fear of being understood.

I am the modest Joe who hems and haws
at blond cashiers ensconced in ticket booths.

Lacking the words to offer her the flowers
I'd spent a fortnight locating the words

to offer her, I threw the flowers at her.
As penance, I entrenched you, Doll, in wood.

Through your shaved bark and twigs, you stared at me.
Being a woman was out of the question.

Being a question caused women to wonder.
How unrestrained you must feel, Wind and Water.

You are the obligation, Box, to harbor
each disarray and ghost. I am the author,

the authored by. I am a plaything of.
Who makes whom Spectacle. Who gives whom Order.

My father was a man who lived and died.
He would commute from Nyack to New York.

The woolen business had its ups and downs.
How unrestrained you've become, Cage and Coffin.

There is an order to each spectacle.
You are the obligation, Wind, to sunder

this relic of. Am reliquary for
the off-white light of January morning.

Have seen you, Fairies, in your apricot
and chestnut negligees invade the mirror,

tiptoe on marbles, vanish from the scene.
Am reliquary for what World has seen.

I'm the ballet of wingspan, the cracked mirror.
Canary's coffin. Sunshine breaking through.

Psalm

My, what incredible gods breathe inside us.
Do you remember the laughter?
Breezelusty, moonswept, the Mediterranean
laps the basalt we carve voices from.
Somebody vows he will finish a book,
the Big Book of Feuds, of stuck pages, the one he is reading.
Somebody forecasts a courtyard and stucco.
There will be a fountain. He will have swans.
Somebody knows he will swim to Nepal,
assemble a porch swing in San Bernardino,
cast one more chicken at several dead whores.
Who is it suggests that we fire the first salvo
at the stone fort, get it over with.
There are no tires rolling into crowds,
these are good times, good times, good times,
we are incredible. Gods breathe inside us.
The wireless, dutiful, advises you:
People of Malta Have Sunk Into Apathy,
while here, near foghorns, on the Isle of Dogs,
disputes over smuggled coffee continue.

The
Juniper
Prize

This volume is the 32nd recipient
of the Juniper Prize for Poetry
presented annually by the University
of Massachusetts Press for a volume
of original poetry. The prize is
named in honor of Robert Francis
(1901–1987), who lived for many
years at Fort Juniper, Amherst,
Massachusetts.